PUFFIN BOOKS

A Monster of a Hamster

Elizabeth Hawkins lives in London and Dorset. She
has written a number of books for children of all
ages and she also teaches and lectures on writing for
children.

Elizabeth Hawkins

A Monster of a Hamster

Illustrated by Mike Terry

PUFFIN BOOKS

For James Barnes

PUFFIN BOOKS

Published by the Penguin Group
Penguin Books Ltd, 27 Wrights Lane, London W8 5TZ, England
Penguin Books USA Inc., 375 Hudson Street, New York, New York 10014, USA
Penguin Books Australia Ltd, Ringwood, Victoria, Australia
Penguin Books Canada Ltd, 10 Alcorn Avenue, Toronto, Ontario, Canada M4V 3B2
Penguin Books (NZ) Ltd, 182–190 Wairau Road, Auckland 10, New Zealand

Penguin Books Ltd, Registered Offices: Harmondsworth, Middlesex, England

First published in Puffin Books 1997

5 7 9 10 8 6

Text copyright © Elizabeth Hawkins, 1997
Illustrations copyright © Mike Terry, 1997
All rights reserved

The moral right of the author and illustrator has been asserted

Filmset in Baskerville MT

Made and printed in England by Clays Ltd, St Ives plc

British Library Cataloguing in Publication Data
A CIP catalogue record for this book is available from the British Library

ISBN 0–140–38124–4

Contents

Contents

1 No School on Monday

"QUIET, CHILDREN!" BELLOWED Mr Pigott. "Now what do we have to remember on Monday?"

The shouting that broke out from Class 3 of Hopswood Junior School shook the sprouting beans on the science table and sent the terrified hamster diving under the hay in his cage.

Mr Pigott was new this term. How he had got through his exams to be a teacher was a mystery to Luke. The dumbest teacher knew not to ask a question of the whole class.

Mr Pigott waved his arms up and down like some bird that had forgotten how to fly.

"Luke Jones! Luke, ARE YOU LISTENING?"

"Who, me, Mr Pigott?"

"Come on, Luke. You tell me. Make it sharp now or the whole class will stay in after school."

Mr Pigott grinned happily.

The sudden silence was deafening. Every one knew it was the third episode of *The Monster's Revenge* on telly after school. The thought of missing it would have silenced an angel choir, let alone Class 3.

"The answer, Luke?" said Mr Pigott grimly, stroking his beard.

"What's the question, Mr Pigott? I mean, you can't expect me to hear with all this din. I mean, that's not fair, is it?"

In front of him Anna-Louise shook her ginger curls over the back of her chair and smiled sweetly, "Mr Pigott asked: What do we have to remember on Monday?"

"Anna-Louise. I am not talking to you," boomed Mr Pigott.

"Monday, Pig," mumbled Luke, "I mean Mr Pigott, it's a bank holiday. We don't have to come to school."

"At last, Luke! I shall not have to look at your miserable face on Monday. NO ONE is to come to school."

"Yippee!" yelled one of the twins. He was shushed and immediately pounced on by the other twin and pushed under the table.

The monster was going to break into the castle for its revenge tonight and no one intended to miss a single, spine-chilling minute.

"One more thing," bellowed Mr Pigott

at the squirming children. "I don't suppose that a miracle could have taken place in this class of television zombies . . ."

Luke stared at Mr Pigott in agony. Mr Pigott was keeping them in to spoil their fun, Luke was sure of it.

"Would it be too much to hope that a kind, generous child would take the hamster home for the holiday? It will

only take ten minutes to give you the instructions."

The silence was as thick as treacle.

"I thought not. How could a class of TV-crazed hooligans care for a lonely creature . . .?"

Luke looked at his Superhero jungle watch. Seven minutes, thirty-two seconds to go till *The Monster's Revenge* started.

"I will, Mr Pigott," said Anna-Louise. "I'll look after him, then he won't be lonely will he? And Luke, you'll stay behind and help me carry the cage, won't you, Luke?"

2 *Take That Rat Away!*

ANNA-LOUISE HAD been born good
like everyone else, at least so Luke
reckoned, but unlike everyone else she
had never learnt anything different.

Luke knew that because he had lived
next door to Anna-Louise since they
were both babies.

Anna-Louise never pinched people, or
borrowed things without asking, or said
unkind things about other children.
This was odd enough, but oddest of all,
despite all this goodness, Anna-Louise
was always getting into trouble.

"Why did you have to ask for the

hamster?" puffed Luke, as he and
Anna-Louise struggled down the road
with the cage.

"I didn't ask for it," gasped Anna-
Louise. "Nobody wanted it. How would
you like to be unwanted and alone all
holiday in an empty classroom?"

"It wouldn't have noticed. Hamsters
sleep all day. Mr Pigott might have

taken him home himself, if you'd kept quiet. What's the time?"

It had taken more than ten minutes to hear what hamsters ate, how much water they liked and how the cage door must always be kept shut.

"I bet we've missed *The Monster's Revenge* . . . all for a sleeping hamster that couldn't care less."

"Oh Luke," wailed Anna-Louise. "It's all my fault. But it's not too late. We can catch the end of *The Monster's Revenge* at my house."

When Luke and Anna-Louise reached the shiny, green door of Anna-Louise's house they knocked hopefully.

At the sight of Luke and the hamster cage, the smile on Anna-Louise's mother's face bounced back like a rubber band. Luke might have guessed.

"What have you brought that rat

home for?" she shrieked. She pulled a neatly ironed, white handkerchief from her apron pocket and held it over her nose. "I will not have a rat in my clean kitchen," she snuffled.

Anna-Louise's kitchen was much cleaner than Luke's kitchen. It was the sort of kitchen you were only allowed to walk around in socks in case your shoes made the floor dirty. Anna-Louise had no little brothers and sister to mess it up and her mother was always cleaning it.

Anna-Louise's mother sniffed the cage.

"I knew it! It smells! A . . . a . . . tchoo! Take it away – a . . . a . . . tchoo! I'm allergic to rats."

The hamster woke up at the sneezing and rattled all over the cage with fright.

"What are we going to do with it?" said Luke glumly as Anna-Louise's

mother slammed the green door shut.

"I don't know," said Anna-Louise
sadly. "We could put it on the lawn."

"Your mother is sure to see it from the
living room windows. I bet she'd
murder it or something."

"She wouldn't, Luke!" said Anna-
Louise. "At least, I don't think so," she
added uncertainly.

"I know . . . why don't we put it
behind the dustbins," said Luke. "Your

mother doesn't like dustbins so she won't hang about there looking for anything."

So they squeezed the cage into the gap between the dustbins and the fence.

For the second time Anna-Louise and Luke knocked at the shiny, green door. It opened a crack.

"I hope you are well rid of that filthy

vermin," said Anna-Louise's mother.

Anna-Louise smiled her sweetest smile. "Luke helped me. Can he stay and watch *The Monster's Revenge* with me?"

"You're certainly not watching that rubbish. Besides it's *Gardener's Delight* on the other channel and I'm watching that."

What a miserable day, thought Luke, as the door closed behind Anna-Louise. First Mr Pigott, then Anna-Louise and finally her mother had ruined the treat he'd waited all week for. All the class would be talking about *The Monster's Revenge* after the holiday and he wouldn't have seen it.

Luke went home the quickest way. He climbed on to the dustbins, shinned over the fence and leapt down into his back garden. He could hear the hamster scrabbling in the cage from the other side of the fence.

"It's all your fault," he hissed through the hole he and Anna-Louise had made when they were little. "You're . . . you're a monster. That's what you are."

3 Escaped!

LUKE DIDN'T SEE Anna-Louise over
the weekend.

He and his family went to visit his
Grandpa and then on Monday they
went to the bank holiday fair on the
recreation field. Most of his friends
were there too, but not Anna-Louise.
Her mother thought fairs were too dirty
and crowded.

That night Luke arrived home late.

Would Anna-Louise's mother have
discovered the hamster? He'd better
check. Mr Pigott had said that he
would hold Luke and Anna-Louise

jointly responsible for the hamster. It could be difficult explaining away a murder.

Luke climbed over the back fence, landed on the dustbin and peered down into the dark. He reached down his hand and felt the cold bars of the cage. It was all quiet, except for the screech of the wobbly dustbin as he straightened up.

On Tuesday morning, Luke woke slowly.

"Luke, how many times do I have to call you?" shouted his father from the foot of the stairs.

On weekends and holidays Luke was the first up, but as soon as school started he got his old sleeping sickness back.

After breakfast Luke went round and knocked on Anna-Louise's green door. The door opened a crack.

"Is Anna-Louise ready?" he asked.

"She's taking that revolting rat back to school," came a muffled voice through the crack. "It will be the death of me if I so much as smell it."

The door slammed shut.

Luke found Anna-Louise behind the dustbins. She looked terrible.

"You look terrible, Anna-Louise! You're not going to cry, are you?"

"Look. It's gone," Anna-Louise groaned.

Luke looked in the cage, turned over the bedding and then shook the cage upside down. Anna-Louise was right – no hamster.

"But it couldn't possibly have escaped, Anna-Louise. Mr Pigott especially showed us how to latch the door shut."

Anna-Louise sniffed.

"I mean, hamsters can't chew through metal bars . . ." Luke's voice faded away. Visions of murder unfurled before him. "Your mother —" he whispered.

"No . . . no . . ." moaned Anna-Louise.

"But this is a cage, Anna-Louise, like

a prison cell. A hamster couldn't break out of it."

"That's just the point, Luke," whimpered Anna-Louise. "How would you like to be locked in a metal prison cell, stuck behind a dustbin, surrounded by smelly bags of rubbish, nothing to see, nowhere to play . . ."

Slowly the light dawned on Luke.

"You didn't . . . you didn't let it out, did you Anna-Louise?"

Anna-Louise nodded slowly.

"Everyone went to the fair yesterday. I had no one to play with and the hamster had no one to play with, so I thought . . ." Anna-Louise's voice trailed away.

Luke examined the dustbins. They were no longer on their concrete base. Someone had laid grass and twigs and leafy branches over the concrete. In the middle sat a silver pie plate from the rubbish, filled with water, like a miniature lake.

"What's all this?" demanded Luke. Anna-Louise's mother would never allow such a mess.

"It's a safari park," whispered Anna-Louise. "It was for the hamster. I spent ages making it and he loved it, he really did."

"Did your mother allow it?"

"She doesn't know. She hasn't been out of the house since the hamster came. You should have seen the hamster, Luke. He ran along the branches, hid under the leaves, put his paws –"

"Did you put him back?" asked Luke sharply.

"Sort of. He loved it such a lot . . . I left the cage door open and built a fence of branches and leaves, so that he could have a run but not escape, but,"

Anna-Louise shuddered with a sob, "but someone moved the dustbin in the night."

Luke groaned. He remembered the wobble and the screech.

"What are we going to do, Luke? We'll have to tell Mr Pigott and he'll be cross enough, but my mother will be furious if she knows there's a hamster wandering the garden. She'll die."

Luke had heard Anna-Louise's mother say a lot of things would make her die. She never did.

It was all Anna-Louise's fault. Luke had a good mind to leave it to her to get them out of this mess.

But that wouldn't be any good. Anna-Louise had an imagination the size of a pea. She'd only go and tell and then they would both be in trouble.

"I know," said Luke. "We won't tell your mother or Mr Pigott. Somehow we'll have to think of a way of keeping them both off the scent, until we catch the hamster and get it back to school."

"What will we do with the cage?" said Anna-Louise tearfully.

"We'll stuff something in the hay and say the hamster is sleeping. Your mother will see us carrying away the cage with the hump in and think the hamster has gone."

"But what about Mr Pigott? He's bound to check to see if the hamster is all right."

Luke stared at the empty cage and thought.

"We'll keep him away – until we've had time to make a new one."

"Make a new what?" said Anna-Louise.

"In craft – the first lesson," said Luke excitedly. "We can use plasticine for the body, some yellow wool for fur and

those black beads for eyes . . . a home-made hamster."

"A home-made hamster! Oh Luke, you're a genius," said Anna-Louise, rubbing away a tear on her clean sleeve.

Sometimes, Luke decided, it wasn't all bad helping Anna-Louise.

4 A Pathetic Monster

"GOOD MORNING, ANNA-LOUISE and Luke," said Mr Pigott rubbing his hands together. "Refreshed from the holiday, are we? And good – the hamster is safely back I see. How's it been?"

"Well . . ." said Anna-Louise. "It's sort of . . . well . . ."

"Well, is it – just what I should hope to hear. Let's see how it has survived its little outing."

Anna-Louise almost dropped her end of the cage with fright.

"We'd better put it at the back of the

class, out of the sunlight, Mr Pigott,"
said Luke quickly. "It's asleep, Mr
Pigott. Sometimes holidays can be a bit
tiring."

"That's unusually thoughtful of you,
Luke," smiled Mr Pigott, flashing white
teeth in a scraggy beard. "I see you
have benefited from your holiday too."
The teeth reminded Luke of the
monster.

Luke and Anna-Louise set the cage at
the back of the classroom. Mr Pigott
was in a good mood. With any luck
Luke would be able to keep him away
from the cage.

"Luke," called out Mr Pigott. "Let us
continue your excellent start to the day.
Take the register to the headmistress's
office, and DON'T dawdle on the
way."

Horrors! Luke couldn't leave Anna-
Louise alone. Not only was she

incapable of keeping a secret, but she always ended up telling everyone.

"Ouch!"

"Come along now, Luke. Don't play the fool."

"Sorry, Mr Pigott," gasped Luke, doubled up over his knee. "Hurt my knee on the bumper cars at the fair. Mum says I've got to rest it."

Mr Pigott eyed him suspiciously.

"You were walking perfectly adequately when you carried the hamster's cage into the classroom."

"It was the strain of it, Mr Pigott. It hit me just when I put the cage down."

Mr Pigott stared coldly at Luke and drummed his fingers on the register.

"My mistake, Luke! I thought the little holiday had turned you into a responsible, caring boy. But," Mr Pigott's voice was working up like a steam engine, "you're the same unruly,

wretch of a boy underneath. Right . . .
who'll take the register?"

Anna-Louise's hand started to go up,
but Luke snatched it down.

"As I have so many offers," bellowed
Mr Pigott, "I will have to choose. Twins
– you can't hide behind the door. You
can take it."

Mr Pigott handed over the register to
the twins.

Delia and David looked alike. They
both had shiny, blond hair and baby
big, blue eyes. With their big eyes and
wide smiles they looked so innocent,
that no grown-up would believe the
terrible behaviour they were capable of.

Luke found an empty table in the
corner for Anna-Louise and himself.
He wasn't going to have anyone
watching what they were up to.

"For craft this morning," began

Mr Pigott in a voice loud enough to fill a football pitch let alone Class 3, "I would like you to make that monster you were all rushing off to see on television before the holiday. In the boxes in front of you, you will find wood, scraps of materials, empty egg boxes and lavatory rolls, beads and buttons. The best will go on show for Parents' Evening."

There were shouts of "Wow!" and "Fantastic!"

"But we missed *The Monster's Revenge*," moaned Anna-Louise to Luke. "I can't remember what the monster looks like."

"Shut up!" hissed Luke. "We've got to make the hamster."

"Luke, DO NOT TALK. Ah, twins – you're back. Luke and Anna-Louise have room on their table. I'm sure you

can set a better example to Anna-Louise than Luke."

"What are you making, Luke?" asked David, as his monster fell apart for the second time.

Anna-Louise opened her mouth, but saw Luke's scowl just in time. She went on carefully sticking bits of yellow wool to the plasticine body Luke had modelled.

Luke selected two shiny black beads and pushed them in for the eyes.

"That's a pathetic monster," said David. "It looks more like a mouse."

"I don't expect their mothers let them watch *The Monster's Revenge*," muttered Delia, as her toilet roll serpent rolled off the table for the seventh time. "Too frightening. I expect they watched *Gardener's Delight* or something."

"Shut up!" whispered Luke, as fiercely

as he dared. He was longing to ask if the monster got his revenge but he couldn't risk Mr Pigott coming over now.

"Right. Are you ready?" he whispered to Anna-Louise.

Anna-Louise went as pale as a ghost. To the twins' astonishment, she dropped to her knees and crawled along the floor. Luke followed carrying the plasticine hamster in his hand.

The twins' eyes opened as wide as full moons. This looked like something too good to miss, so they too dropped to the floor.

"Get off! We don't want you," whispered Luke hoarsely. "You'll get us caught."

Anna-Louise had reached the cage. With shaking hands she undid the latch.

"Luke's table – why do I have to keep

. . . what IS going on?" boomed Mr Pigott.

Luke stuck his hand through the open door of the cage and pushed the hamster into the hay, until just its nose and beady eyes stuck out.

The twins' eyes were the size of saucers.

"Where are they? Where is Luke's table? I'm not having this –"

Mr Pigott's voice was approaching like machine-gun fire.

Delia's shining hair and blue eyes appeared above the edge of the table.

"It's Luke's fault," whined Delia. "He knocked my serpent off the table. We can't find it anywhere."

"Here it is!" David shouted, as his wide grin appeared above the table beside Delia. In his hand he held Delia's battered serpent.

"Well done, David," said Mr Pigott.

"Now get up all of you. And any more nonsense from you Luke, and you'll be spending the rest of the day outside the headmistress's office."

5 A Nasty Discovery

"WHAT HAPPENED IN *The Monster's Revenge?*" asked Luke eagerly, when he and David got out into the playground.

"I'm not going through all that," said David. "You should have watched it yourself. Why did you put your monster in the hamster's cage?"

"Even a hamster wouldn't be frightened of a pathetic mouse like that," added Delia.

"It's not a mouse," said Anna-Louise indignantly. "It's a hamster."

David and Delia laughed loudly.

"No, it's not. It's a cross between a

miniature, hairy mammoth and a
smelly, rubber ball," said Delia.

Luke saw that the whole thing was
getting out of hand. The twins
wouldn't be able to resist telling the
other children and then Mr Pigott

would hear. There wasn't much choice about it, he decided unhappily. He'd have to tell the twins and let them in on the secret.

"Promise not to tell."

"Course we won't."

"Cross your heart and hope to die."

The twins fell to the ground, dead.

"All right then."

Luke whispered the whole story hurriedly to them. "So if we can pretend to feed it without Mr Pigott going near it, we'll have longer to catch the real hamster."

"Amazing," said David.

"We'll help," said Delia.

The remainder of the day passed peacefully enough with Maths, P.E. and Story Writing. Class 3 were busy writing stories about the monster they had made.

Delia wrote about a serpent that only ate girls with red hair and she kept showing it to Anna-Louise.

David chewed his pencil and wrote one line: "Once upon a time, there was this monster", and got stuck there.

Luke wanted to write about the monster in *The Monster's Revenge*, but he didn't know what had happened. Instead he wrote about a monster that hid behind a green kitchen door and pounced out on passing girls and boys. The monster also happened to be afraid of rats.

Anna-Louise wrote a whole page in her best writing about a monster that looked like a miniature, hairy mammoth and smelt of rubber balls, but which was really a . . .

"You can't write that," said Luke, as he peered over her elbow. "Mr Pigott will guess. Tear it up."

"But it's the best story I've ever written," said Anna-Louise sadly.

"Go on, tear it up," ordered Delia.

The tearing sound ripped through the quiet classroom.

"What ARE you doing, Anna-Louise?" came a bellow from Mr Pigott.

"I'm tearing up my story, Mr Pigott."

"Did you say – TEARING IT UP?"

"It was a rotten story," said David helpfully.

"What a very SILLY thing to do, Anna-Louise. I hope it wasn't one of these silly, rude stories," said Mr Pigott smiling nastily. "But never mind. You can look forward to a pleasant evening tonight writing it all out again. At least four pages."

Mr Pigott stood up, looking much less cheerful than he had at the beginning of the day.

"Before EVERYONE packs up, whose turn is it to feed the hamster?"

Hands shot up on all sides. Luke pushed his way forward, waving his arm.

"Luke! Stop pushing! You and Anna-Louise had the hamster all through the holiday, but do you think of giving another child a turn? No, you don't. NO, LUKE. If I say NO, I mean NO. Now, what about Samantha? Ali? Ben? How shall I choose?"

The twins stood quietly at the back blinking their big, round eyes and smiling their widest smiles.

"Ah! David and Delia! Look at them, children. David and Delia have already, and without waiting to be asked, cleared their places and put their books away."

The class stared at them in surprise.

"So David and Delia it shall be."

If it was to be anyone it was best it was them, thought Luke with relief. Thank goodness he had let them in on the secret.

As the other children cleared their tables, David and Delia emptied the hamster's water bottle and filled it with fresh water. Then they filled up the nut and seed tray, and added fresh hay.

"It's all going to be all right, Anna-Louise," said Luke happily.

"Oh Luke, I don't usually like boys, but you're the best one I –"

Luke didn't hear the rest. A scream as good as any in *The Monster's Revenge* smothered Anna-Louise's words. It was followed by a loud sobbing from the back of the classroom.

"Delia, what is it?" called Mr Pigott. "David – are you all right?"

There was another scream and a few

more sobs as David struggled to speak.

"The hamster –" he sobbed.

"– It's dead!" wailed Delia.

Luke clasped his head in his hands. Why had he told them? Why had he ever thought he could trust them?

6 A Funeral

"DEATH," SAID MR Pigott, "is a most sad occasion."

A sob went up from Delia. It was catching. Samantha sniffed and Ali wiped his eyes on his football shirt.

"But animals, like humans, must die when they are old," went on Mr Pigott, delighted for once to have everyone listening. "It is part of life's natural cycle."

"What's he talking about?" said Anna-Louise with a worried frown.

"Old bicycles, I think," said Luke miserably.

The storm would break out any minute now, when the plasticine hamster was discovered. There was nothing he could do about it.

The children were pushing and shoving into the corner to see the dead hamster.

Ali poked his finger between the bars and into the hay.

"Ooh . . . it's cold and sort of sticky."

"It must have been dead a while if it's cold," said Delia.

"It's going rotten, that's why it's sticky," said David. "Dead things do, don't they Mr Pigott, like monsters?"

Luke couldn't wait to get Delia and David out in the playground. They would be cold and sticky by the time he'd finished with them.

"Thank you Delia and David," said Mr Pigott, "but that's quite enough. A sad end to our day, children, but it is

time to go home. I will ask the
caretaker to dispose of the . . . er . . .
corpse."

"Dispose of the corpse!" sobbed
Samantha. "You can't throw out our
lovely hamster like a bit of old rubbish.
What about a funeral?"

"Yeah," yelled Ben. "Let's have a
funeral."

"There's nothing good on telly
tonight," added Ali helpfully.

Luke tried to shut his ears to the
shouts going up on all sides in favour of
staying late for a funeral.

Samantha volunteered to tell the
waiting parents in the playground.

"It's not every day you get a death in
the classroom," said Delia cheerfully.

Mr Pigott looked delighted with the
children's enthusiasm. Never before
had the children volunteered to stay
late after school. Funeral announcements

51

were designed on white paper with black pens. Floral wreaths were drawn on coloured paper.

"Luke," said Mr Pigott. "Not helping I see! You can take this note to the headmistress asking her to join us at the funeral. Let her see the quality of my class. And I don't want to hear a word about your knee. I saw you playing football in the lunch-break."

Mr Pigott straightened his tie and smoothed down his beard.

"Anna-Louise, don't look so shocked, dear. Believe me, I share your sorrow. Forget the monster story tonight and sit down now and write us a little poem about the hamster. You can read it over the grave."

Luke arrived back in time to see David nd Delia dive into the hamster's cage a spotted, pirate scarf from the drama box. They re-emerged with a neatly wrapped, spotted bundle.

Ali found an empty chalk box for a coffin. He decorated the sides with drawings of spaceships.

"So that its soul can travel out of this world in a spaceship. It's quicker than angels."

Soon the funeral party was ready.

Delia walked solemnly at the front carrying the spaceship coffin. Samantha sobbed behind her.

The children shuffled and jumped along, some giggling, some sniffing. Mr Pigott and the headmistress took up the rear with solemn expressions, broken only to stare sternly at Luke, who was trying to stamp on David's foot.

Last of all, the waiting parents followed the procession to the school garden.

"What a lovely, caring school," said a

mother, as she blew her nose hard with her handkerchief.

David dug a hole among the sunflowers. Delia and Samantha laid in the coffin. Mr Pigott stood back and waved Anna-Louise forward.

Anna-Louise took a deep breath and read:

> "We had a hamster
> But he went away.
> Perhaps he'll come back
> One sunny day."

"Lovely," said Mr Pigott very loudly
so the headmistress could hear.
"Beautifully written. But Anna-Louise,
things don't come back when they're
dead, do they?"

7 It's Not Over Yet

"WHAT DID YOU do that for?" shouted Luke to David, as Luke, Anna-Louise and the twins set off down the road home.

"It was brilliant!" said Delia.

"Fantastic!" said David.

"But you've ruined everything," groaned Luke.

"And I stuck on all those little pieces of wool," said Anna-Louise sadly.

"Anna-Louise has a brain the size of a pea," said Delia.

"And Luke hasn't got one at all," said David. "Like a monster. Don't you see,

Luke – Mr Pigott would have discovered that plasticine, hairy mammoth. You'd have been in bad trouble. Now it's buried, he'll never know Anna-Louise lost the hamster."

"You should say thank you nicely to us for saving you both," said Delia. "Go on Anna-Louise, fall down and kiss my feet."

Anna-Louise looked down at Delia's dirty shoes and wrinkled up her nose.

"All right," said Delia, "you can give me three sweets instead."

Anna-Louise pulled a dusty toffee from her pocket.

"I've only got one."

"Oh no you don't!" said Luke, grabbing the toffee. "We'll need that to tempt the hamster."

"The hamster?"

"You never thought of that, did you?" said Luke fiercely to David and Delia.

"What's going to happen to the hamster running about in Anna-Louise's garden? What are we going to do about that?"

"You shouldn't keep animals in cages," sniffed David.

"That's just what I thought," said Anna-Louise. "I made this lovely safari park . . ."

"It's not a wild animal," said Luke. "It's a pet. How is it going to survive in the wild? It doesn't know how to find its own food or look after itself. It will be killed by the first prowling cat it meets."

"Oh!" said David.

Delia gazed down at her dirty shoes.

"We've got to catch it," said Anna-Louise. "My mum has an allergy to rats and mice and hamsters. She doesn't know the hamster is still in the garden. If she finds it she'll die and complain

to Mr Pigott and make him come and
get it and then there'd be two hamsters
and how would we explain that?"

"We won't have to explain," said
Luke. "We'll catch it."

8 Still Searching

"I'M NOT HAVING all these children in the house, Anna-Louise," said her mother when she opened the shiny, green door. "They'll make my kitchen dirty."

"We're going to play in the garden," said Anna-Louise.

"Half an hour only. Then I want you in for tea – alone."

The green door slammed shut.

Delia took a shoe lace out of her shoe and tied Anna-Louise's toffee to it.

Luke searched in his back pocket for the crumbs of the biscuit he had sat on

the day before. David found a cracked
magnifying glass in his school bag.

"Where did the hamster go, then?"
said Delia.

"I don't know," said Anna-Louise. She
glanced nervously back at the living
room windows. "We could look in the
flower bed."

They dropped a few crumbs, swung
the toffee among the flower stalks and

searched for tiny footprints with the magnifying glass.

"There are hundreds of tiny footprints here," said David. "What are hamster's footprints like?"

"They've got claws," said Luke. They would have to hurry. It wouldn't be long before Anna-Louise's mother checked on what they were up to. "Four claws and –"

Above them, a window sprang open.

"What are you doing in my flowers?" shouted the red face of Anna-Louise's mother. "Look – they're bent. They'll be ruined. Get off the flower bed – at once."

"It's too crowded in here," muttered Luke. "Let's lay a crumb trail on the lawn and tempt the hamster out."

The children scattered the biscuit crumbs across the lawn. No sooner had they got to the other side than the trail was spotted . . . but not by the hamster.

A cooing, a swooping, a flapping descended all around them.

"Look at that!" said David. "There are at least a hundred pigeons."

"A hundred – how do you know?" said Delia.

"I counted them."

"No you didn't."

The green door swung open.

"Get them off!" came a shriek Luke
knew all too well. "They'll mess up my
lawn."

Anna-Louise's mother emerged
banging a saucepan lid.

"Off . . . Off . . . Get off my lawn!"

"That's done it," groaned Luke. "The
hamster will have been frightened to
the other side of the moon by now."

"And as for you children," shouted Anna-Louise's mother. "You leave at once, do you hear. And Luke – I shall have a word to say to your mother. AAH! Look! My lettuces, my spinach."

Luke looked at the vegetable patch. Why was Anna-Louise's mother making such a racket? As far as he could see there wasn't much in the patch apart from a few empty stalks and a half-eaten leaf.

David and Delia were watching with interest. Anna-Louise's mother was crawling on her hands and knees over the bare vegetable patch, examining the stalks and making little screeching noises.

Anna-Louise trembled with fear.

Her mother reached the corner and examined the half-eaten spinach leaf. Then – atchoo! . . . atchoo! . . . atchoo!

Anna-Louise's mother leapt to her

feet, sped down the path, into the house and slammed the door.

"Can we come to your house again?" said Delia admiringly. "Your mother is much more interesting than ours."

"What's wrong with you two?" said David.

Luke was lying face down in the spinach leaves with Anna-Louise collapsed on top of him.

"It's all right, she's gone," said Delia. "You can get up now."

"I can't," said Luke. "It's the hamster . . . it's under my tummy."

9 Secret Plans

IT WAS DECIDED. They would put the hamster in the empty dustbin overnight. Anna-Louise lined it with the remains of her safari park and filled up the silver pie dish with fresh water.

"I'm getting in the council vermin exterminator tomorrow," Anna-Louise overhead her mother say, as she went to wash her hands for tea.

"There's a waiting list, dear," said Anna-Louise's father.

"I have a garden teeming with rats. That rat Anna-Louise brought home from school bred when it was here. I shall insist the exterminator comes at once."

"Yes, dear."

Meanwhile, over the fence, Luke's mother was finishing Luke's peanut-butter sandwiches for his next day's packed lunch.

"I can't find your lunch box, Luke."

"I'll put the sandwiches in."

"No. Give it to me, Luke. I'll wash it."

"I'll wash it."

"No. Give it to me," Luke's mother gasped. "What have you done to it? It's peppered with little holes."

"They're air holes."

"What do you need air holes for?"

"To air his sandwiches. That's obvious," said Luke's father putting his newspaper down. He gave Luke a wink. "Luke probably got attacked by bandits

with machine-guns on his way back from school today."

"He's not getting a new one, that's for sure," said Luke's mother.

However, David and Delia's mother was delighted.

"Playing at Anna-Louise's house? They've got such a lovely house and garden. I'm glad you two are making some nice, polite friends at last."

All three mothers were surprised when, the next morning, Anna-Louise, Luke, David and Delia woke on time and left their homes early for swimming practice.

Luke waited outside Anna-Louise's house. She rushed out clutching her swimming costume in front of her, as if it might leap away at any minute. Round the corner Luke popped the

wriggling swimming costume into his
lunch box.

David and Delia were waiting at the

crossing, leaping about with excitement. Luke wished David and Delia had never got involved. The way David and Delia were carrying on, someone was bound to wonder what they were up to.

"What's that sticking out of your school bag?" said Luke suspiciously.

"A spade, silly," said Delia.

"We're going to dig up the coffin," said David.

10 Breaking In

THE SCHOOL GATES were still locked.

"We'll have to climb over," said Delia.

"It's not allowed," said Anna-Louise anxiously.

But David already had his hands on the KEEP OUT – PRIVATE PROPERTY sign. He hauled himself up and reached the HOPSWOOD JUNIOR SCHOOL – HEADMISTRESS: MRS HARRINGTON; CARETAKER: MR TUMP sign.

With another heave David was over the top and had jumped down on to the other side. Delia followed.

"Here, hold the hamster," said Luke handing his lunch box to Anna-Louise.

Luke was over in a jiffy.

"Pass the box through the bars."

"It won't go," said Anna-Louise.

The bars of the gate were too narrow for the lunch box.

"You'll have to climb over with it."

"I'm not coming. I don't like heights. They make me all dizzy," said Anna-Louise miserably.

Luke, David and Delia stared at Anna-Louise through the bars of the gate.

"Take the hamster out and hand it through, stupid," hissed Delia, "and throw the box over afterwards."

Anna-Louise took the hamster out of the lunch box and passed it through the bars. Then she picked up Luke's lunch box and sent it crashing over the top of the gates.

Delia popped the hamster back in the box and started off across the playground with David.

"What about me?" wailed Anna-Louise.

"Leave her," called David. "We

haven't got time for sissies."

It serves her right, thought Luke, after all the trouble she had caused him.

"Go away . . ." Luke started, but he made the fatal mistake of looking into Anna-Louise's green eyes, brimming with tears.

"Come on Anna-Louise, you can get over," sighed Luke. "Don't look down. There you are . . . put your foot on MRS HARRINGTON. Now jump – I'll catch you."

As Luke lay squashed flat for the second time by Anna-Louise, he asked himself if any hamster could be worth this much agony.

David and Delia were waiting at the class garden. It was quiet. No one was around yet. The school looked quite spooky with no children and no teachers.

David, Delia and Anna-Louise

squatted down by the pile of freshly turned earth. Luke picked up the spade and began gingerly to dig.

"I bet it's turned into a real monster in the night," said Delia. "A vampire could have bitten it and changed it into a vampire hamster."

Luke felt the spade knock against the coffin.

"I've got the chalk box," he yelled. "Look, here are Ali's spaceship drawings."

"They didn't get too near space," said David. "I reckon an angel would have been faster."

Luke opened the lid. To his relief the plasticine hamster was just as they had left it.

"I think it's lovely," said Anna-Louise, fingering the yellow wool she had stuck on its back.

"Go on, you can have it to keep," said

Luke generously.

"Be careful, it might be a vampire," said Delia.

Luke took the hamster out of the lunch box and gently settled it in the chalk box. With care he punched breathing holes with a pencil in the lid. He was just laying the box on the path beside the garden, where every child would see it as they came into school,

when a roar went up behind them.

"Don't move. I've got you," shouted
Mr Tump, the caretaker. "I knew
someone had broken in. I've had phone
calls about vandals climbing over the
gate. You'll catch it!"

Delia and David squeezed in behind
the sunflowers. Luke hid the spade behind
him. Anna-Louise stood rooted to the
spot, her mouth a perfect, round O.

"I don't believe it!" huffed Mr Tump as he panted up. He stared, horrified, at the hamster's chalk box coffin. "What are children today coming to . . . grave robbers!"

11 Big Trouble

ANNA-LOUISE AND LUKE stood alone in front of the class. Mr Pigott sat at his desk with a stern, worried face. The children waited with interest.

The door sprung open and in strode Mrs Harrington, clutching a large, black handbag like armour plating. Without uttering a word she set the handbag with a thump on the floor. Slowly her chill, grey eyes swept the class, lingering on Luke and Anna-Louise.

"Never," she began. "Never in all my time at Hopswood Junior School have we had such a distressing incident.

Digging up the resting place of your dear hamster . . . dear children, what could be a more terrible thing to do? Of course I blame it on too much television and unsuitable programmes. So I shall be sending a letter to all parents advising against any programmes with monsters, ghosts or the like."

A furious whisper broke out among the children.

"Quiet!" ordered Mrs Harrington.

Luke felt the grey eyes settle on him like a cloud, and shivered.

"As for Anna-Louise and Luke, words cannot express my horror. Fortunately you were found in time by Mr Tump, and also I might say by the twins – David and Delia, who had most thoughtfully arrived early to water the sunflowers. I shall of course call your parents and –"

The door swung open a second time and in hobbled Mr Tump, huffing and puffing.

"Look!" he gasped.

In his trembling hands lay the hamster, a real live hamster, busily nibbling a peanut-butter sandwich.

Words failed Mrs Harrington.

"I was going to bury the coffin again," huffed Mr Tump, "when I hears this scrabbling and snuffling. I don't mind telling you I didn't want to open it, but I sees this whisker poking through a hole in the box, and I opens it, and there I sees this creature eating this bit of bread . . ."

The class craned forward eagerly to watch.

Mr Tump snatched the bread from the hamster and sniffed it.

"Peanut-butter sandwich, it is."

All colour drained from Mr Pigott's

face as he stood up shakily and took the hamster.

"It looks like our hamster. Yes, it certainly does."

"It's a miracle, isn't it Mr Pigott?" called out Samantha.

"Probably just a ghost hamster," said Ali.

"It's sleeping sickness," said Delia. "I saw it on television. You think people are dead but they're not. They are in a deep sleep and if you're not careful they get buried . . ."

"Enough, Delia dear," said Mrs Harrington. "You really must not believe everything you see on these dreadful programmes. Now Mr Pigott, your class has wasted enough of my precious time. Next time, only call me for a funeral when you are quite sure there is a need for one."

Mrs Harrington picked up her black

handbag and marched out. Mr Pigott
blushed an angry red.

A happy chattering broke out in the
classroom.

"Be quiet!" bellowed Mr Pigott. "Yes,
Anna-Louise, what is it now?"

"You won't call my mother, will you Mr Pigott?" said Anna-Louise looking like a ghost herself. "Now we've got the hamster back . . ."

"Not this time," said Mr Pigott. "But any more of this nonsense and I will. Now who is going to put the hamster back in its cage?"

Children's arms shot up like a waving forest, except for the corner where Anna-Louise, Luke and the twins sat.

"It worked," grinned Delia.

"It was brilliant," said David.

"Tell me," said Luke. "What happened on *The Monster's Revenge*?"

"There's no point," said David. "You heard what Mrs Harrington said. We'll have to watch *Gardener's Delight* next week."

Luke groaned, "And I haven't even got any lunch. The hamster's eaten my peanut-butter sandwiches. I'll starve."

He would never, ever do anything for Anna-Louise again.

"You mustn't starve, Luke," said Anna-Louise anxiously. "You can have my lunch. I had a big breakfast."

"All of it?" said Delia, her eyes wide with amazement.

"All of it!" said Anna-Louise.

"No," smiled Luke. "We'll share."